For Doug, who is my calm computer fixer, my best friend,
and very handsome on a good hair day.

www.houghtonmifflinbooks.com

The text of this book is set in Cafeteria.

Library of Congress Cataloging-in-Publication Data
Harper, Charise Mericle.
The Monster Show : everything you never knew about monsters / by Charise Mericle Harper.
p. cm.
Summary: Describes the various characteristics of monsters, such as how much they need
to eat to feel full and how some of them can juggle.
ISBN 0-618-38797-8
[1. Monsters—Fiction.] I. Title.
PZ7.H231323Mo 2004   [E]—dc22   2003017710

Printed in Singapore
TWP 10 9 8 7 6 5 4 3 2 1

but it's hard to tell just by looking at them.

If you saw a monster on roller skates, that would be **FUNNY**. If you saw a monster on a bicycle, that would be **FUNNY**.

But if you saw a monster flying a plane, that would be **SCARY**, because monsters don't know how to fly planes.

Most monsters don't have any pets,

but there is a monster who lives in France who has five pet **butterflies** and a friendly **turtle** named Pierre.

Even monsters look **silly** when they

are just wearing **underpants.**

If you bounce on a monster, he might get mad.

If you bounce on a bed, it's safer.

There are monsters who can JUGGLE,

but most people are afraid to go
to monster picnics to watch them.

If a monster eats a chair and a bowl of spaghetti, he won't be **FULL**. If a monster eats a car filled with peanuts, he won't be **FULL**.

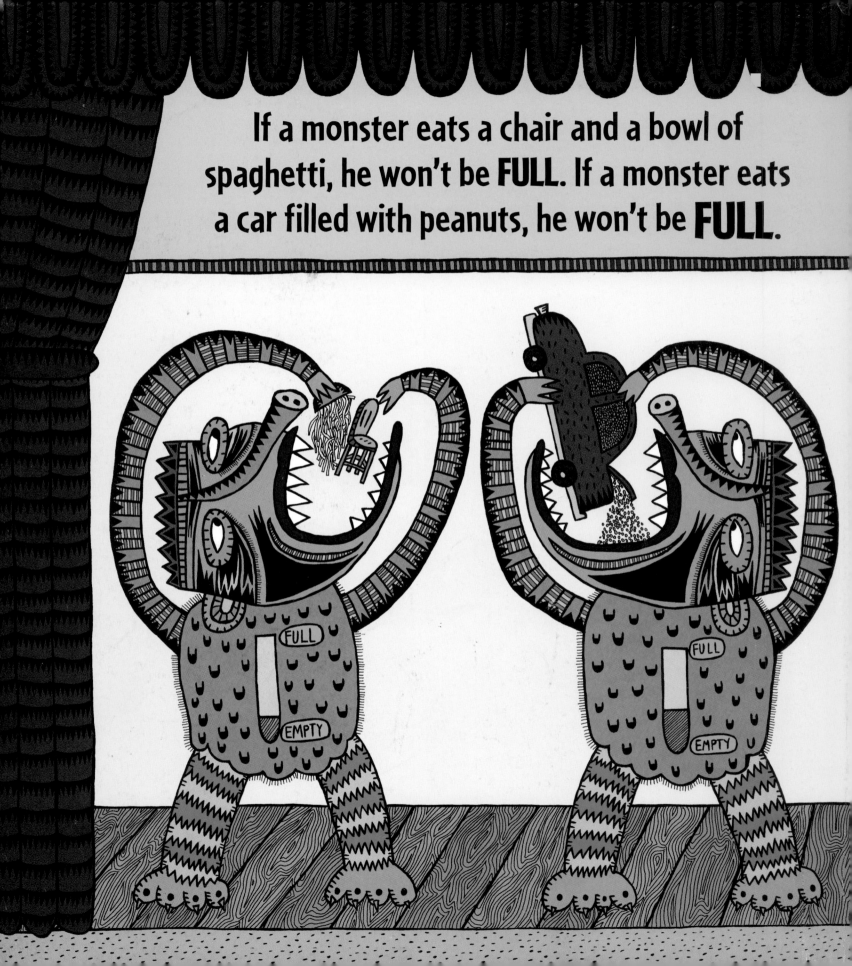

But if a monster eats forty-three pizzas, two boats filled with ice cream, and sixty-two socks, then he might be **FULL**.

Some monsters like to eat toothpaste.

They are the ones with the
MINTY FRESH
breath and the white pointy teeth.

When monsters sleep, they sometimes

about visiting new monsters on other planets.

Monsters don't usually make very good pets,

Not all monsters like the dark.
Daylight monsters have to work harder,

because it's easier to be scary at night.

Most monsters like to have
SINGING SNAKES

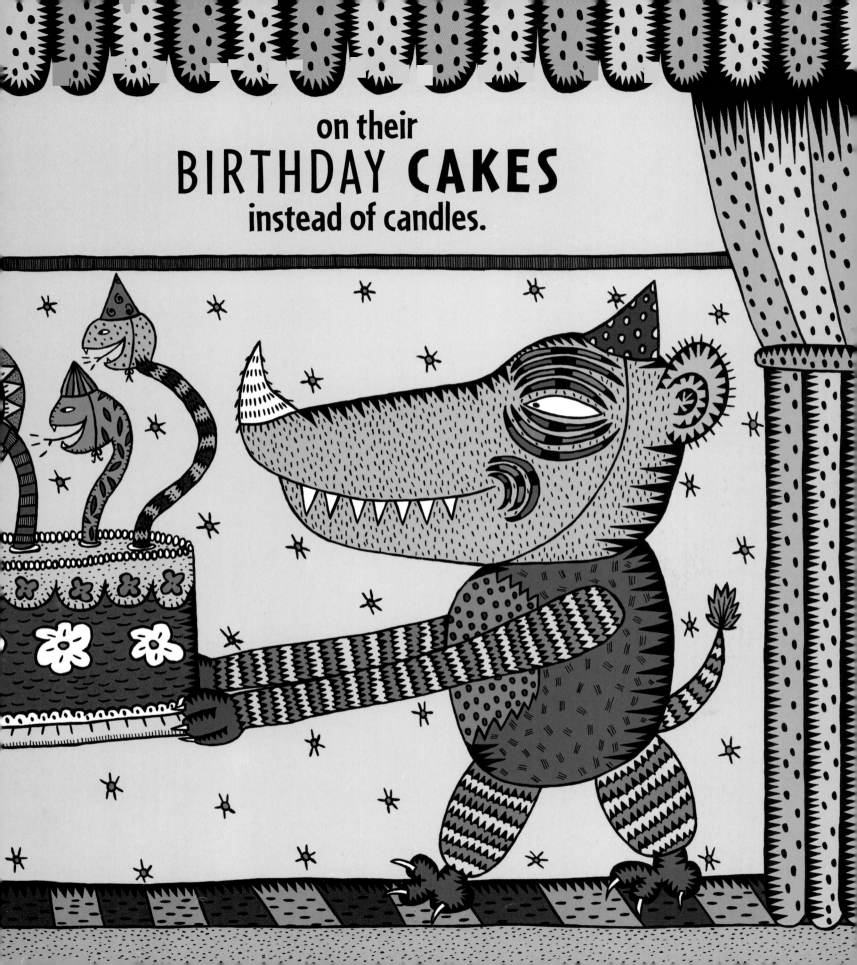

All monsters like to
perform
in front of an audience,

even if that audience is just one person.